Awaken

nadeerashi and Nadeera Goonetilleke

Published by Nadeera Goonetilleke, 2024.

AWAKEN

NADEERA GOONETILLEKE

Copyright Page

Awaken

Transformation, Strength, and New Beginnings

This is a work of fiction. Similarities to real people, places, or events are entirely coincidental.

AWAKEN

First edition. November 21, 2024.

ISBN: 979-8227797469

Written by nadeerashi and Nadeera Goonetilleke.

Event 1

The Final Choice

Richard Thompson, the esteemed Chairman and Managing Director of **Thompson & Co. Marketing Solutions**, was known for his meticulous nature. His company was a powerhouse in the marketing world, synonymous with innovation and prestige.

On this brisk morning, Richard was to personally conduct the initial round of interviews for a Marketing Executive position. This was no small matter for him—Richard had a precise vision for the type of people who would fit seamlessly into the dynamic culture of his company.

The sun had barely risen when Richard arrived at the office. His assistant greeted him with a warm smile, handing him a steaming cup of his favorite dark roast coffee. He savored a quick sip, appreciating its bold aroma before setting it down. After glancing at his watch, he took a deep breath. The day was going to be a marathon, but he thrived on these moments. With a determined stride, he walked into the interview hall. Ten candidates, a mix of men and women, all sat on the edge of their seats, visibly nervous yet hopeful.

"Let's begin," Richard thought as he signaled the receptionist to send in the first candidate.

Candidate 1: Michael Harris

Michael walked in confidently, dressed sharply in a charcoal suit. His eyes revealed a hint of anxiety, but he held his composure.

"Good morning, Mr. Harris. Make yourself comfortable," Richard greeted, holding up his CV. He retrieved it from the file Rachel, his secretary, had handed him the previous evening, where she had carefully numbered the candidates in the order they were to be called.

"Good morning, Mr. Thompson," Michael replied, adjusting his tie.

"So, Michael, tell me why you want to join Thompson & Co. Marketing Solutions?"

Michael leaned slightly forward. "Sir, your company is known for groundbreaking marketing campaigns. I've admired how you managed the 'Reignite' campaign last year—it was innovative and brought significant traction to your client. I'd like to be part of such impactful work."

Richard nodded thoughtfully. "Impressive knowledge. Now, let's get to the heart of it. What marketing strategy would you propose for a brand struggling with consumer engagement in a highly competitive market?"

Michael took a deep breath. "First, I'd perform a thorough market analysis to identify pain points. Based on that, I'd create a campaign that resonates emotionally with the target audience, emphasizing storytelling. Incorporating social media influencers and customer engagement through interactive content would be key."

Richard scribbled some notes. "Interesting. What about your background? Where are you from?"

"I'm from Boston, sir. I come from a middle-class family; my father runs a small business, and my mother is a schoolteacher."

Richard leaned back, assessing. Michael had potential—a mix of ambition and stability.

Candidate 2: Olivia Brooks

Next was Olivia Brooks. She walked in with an air of quiet confidence, dressed professionally but without any pretense.

"Ms. Brooks, good morning," Richard greeted, offering her a seat.

"Good morning, Mr. Thompson. Thank you for this opportunity."

"Olivia, let's cut to the chase. What do you believe makes a marketing campaign memorable?"

Olivia didn't miss a beat. "Authenticity, sir. Audiences can sense when they are being manipulated or sold to without sincerity. A memorable campaign understands and respects its audience while evoking genuine emotion or a call to action."

Richard raised an eyebrow. "What would you do differently if you found that a campaign wasn't producing the expected results?"

"I'd pivot quickly, sir. Acknowledge what isn't working, analyze why, and refocus on alternative strategies while staying aligned with the brand's core message."

"Very well. Where are you based?"

"Currently, I live in Chicago. My family has been there for generations—my father works in IT, and my mother is a freelance writer."

Richard made another note. Olivia was a solid candidate—smart, composed, and articulate. He put a star next to her name.

After concluding several more interviews, Richard had narrowed his choices to Michael and Olivia. Feeling satisfied, he decided it was time for a break. He buzzed the intercom to speak with the receptionist about wrapping up. The line was busy. He tried again and again, but it was constantly engaged. Irritated, he rose from his chair and stepped out.

To his surprise, the receptionist, Emma, was deep in a serious conversation with someone, her head bowed and unaware of Richard's presence. His frustration simmered, but it quickly dissipated when he noticed a young woman seated quietly in a far corner of the hall. She had been there the entire time, waiting patiently without a hint of restlessness.

Intrigued, Richard walked over. "Miss, would you please come in?"

The young woman stood up, her simple attire contrasting sharply with the formal business attire of the other candidates. There was no arrogance or desperation in her demeanor—just a calm, determined presence.

Richard motioned for her to sit as he sat down behind his desk. "I don't believe I have your name. It seems my secretary may have overlooked your application. Could you please share your CV with me?"

Anna paused briefly, then responded with a confident smile, "I'm Anna Wells. If my application was overlooked, I completely understand—things can get hectic. Here's my CV, Mr. Thompson.

"Why didn't you speak up when everyone else was being called?"

"I believed you would notice, sir, eventually," Anna replied softly, a hint of a smile on her lips.

Richard raised an eyebrow, a subtle smile playing at the corners of his mouth. Miss Wells, let's see if your expectations match the reality."

Event 2

The Hidden Gem

Richard leaned back in his chair, observing her composed posture. She wore a simple, modest dress and held a plain leather-bound folder. Unlike the other candidates, there was nothing ostentatious or showy about her. Yet, an undeniable air of quiet confidence surrounded her, and that intrigued Richard.

"Let's begin," he said, adjusting his glasses slightly. "Tell me about yourself, Anna. I'd like to hear about your family background and who you are, in your own words."

Anna offered a faint smile, her eyes locking with his, exuding a blend of sincerity and quiet strength. "Of course, Mr. Thompson. I'm from a small town called Evergreen Hills, where my parents have run a modest bakery for decades. My father starts his day before dawn, baking fresh bread and pastries, while my mother manages the customers and keeps the books. I grew up helping out whenever I could, learning the importance of hard work and community support early on. My younger brother is still in school, and my parents have always placed a strong emphasis on education for both of us."

Richard nodded, genuinely impressed. "That's a rich background in terms of values. But what about you, Anna? What brings you here?"

Anna leaned forward slightly, her voice steady yet filled with ambition. "I've always been captivated by the power of communication and persuasion, sir. Even as a child in the bakery, I saw how subtle details—like a thoughtful greeting or an innovative display—could make a lasting impact on customers. This sparked my passion for marketing. Over the past year, I've been with a small local firm, which has been rewarding, but I've reached the point where I feel my potential is limited. I'm ready for larger campaigns and the opportunity to work with a broader, more diverse clientele. That's where I see my skills truly evolving."

Richard noticed the determined glint in her eyes and the calculated confidence in her tone. She wasn't just seeking a job; she was aiming for growth, eager to prove herself in a bigger arena.

Richard tapped his pen against his notebook. "I see. A valid reason for moving on. Now, let's talk business. Imagine a scenario—our client is facing a steep decline in market share for a product they heavily invested in. What would your first steps be?"

Anna's eyes sparkled with focus. "The first step would be diagnostics, sir. I'd analyze sales data, customer feedback, and competitor strategies to identify what might be causing the decline. Is it poor positioning? Is the product outdated? Perhaps there's a lack of trust with the target audience. Once the core issue is identified, I'd recommend a rebranding effort or product refresh, emphasizing transparency and customer engagement."

Her response was fluid, logical, and grounded in reality. Richard leaned forward, intrigued. "And if you were tasked with managing a high-pressure product launch on a tight deadline, what would be your approach?"

"Teamwork and clear communication would be paramount, Mr. Thompson. I'd break the launch plan into small, actionable steps, assign tasks based on strengths, and implement regular checkpoints to monitor progress. It's crucial to keep stakeholders informed and agile, allowing quick pivots if necessary."

Richard's pen paused mid-note. He stared at Anna for a few moments, feeling a surge of admiration. She spoke with a conviction that belied her limited experience. Her answers were not just theoretical; they were rooted in practicality and awareness.

"Impressive," he said, maintaining his businesslike tone. "Now, tell me, what does marketing mean to you?"

Anna hesitated for a heartbeat, considering her words. "Marketing, sir, is more than just selling a product. It's about connecting with people, understanding their needs and desires, and offering solutions that genuinely make their lives better. It's about trust, integrity, and creativity."

The room fell silent. Richard was spellbound. He saw a spark in Anna that set her apart from everyone else he had interviewed that day. She had intelligence, passion, and a natural ability to see the bigger picture.

Richard jotted down a note with a flourish. "Thank you, Anna. I believe that concludes our interview. We will let you know the results soon."

Her expression remained polite and composed. "Thank you for your time, Mr. Thompson."

As she exited the room, Richard watched her go. He picked up the phone and dialed the marketing manager's extension. "Hi Sam, I selected three candidates. However out of three I think Anna Wells may just be what we need. But you have a second interview and tell me your views. I will send across the applications with my remarks.

But he kept his tone with Anna neutral and withheld any promises. Professionalism and impartiality had always been his creed. Little did she know, she had already made an indelible mark.

A few minutes later, Richard, still sitting behind his polished desk, buzzed the intercom to call the receptionist into his office. He needed to address her uncharacteristic lapse during the interview process—a situation that had left one of the candidates waiting far longer than necessary.

Luna hesitated for a moment before entering, her usual calm demeanor replaced by a nervous, almost guilty look. As she walked in, her eyes darted briefly to the floor, avoiding Richard's steady gaze.

"Come in, Luna," Richard said, his voice professional but firm. He motioned for her to take a seat, his fingers tapping lightly on the desk as he adjusted his tie. "I need to speak with you about what happened earlier. You let one of our candidates wait for an extended period during the interview process. That's not acceptable."

Luna swallowed hard, clearly distressed by the reprimand. She could feel the weight of Richard's gaze on her, his professionalism radiating from his every word. But there was something more in his voice—an underlying seriousness that came from a place of genuine concern for the efficiency and smooth functioning of the office.

"Sir, I—I sincerely apologize," Luna began, her voice trembling slightly as she explained herself. "My brother... he was involved in a bike accident this morning. The bike got damaged badly, but thank God, he's okay. He's been shaken up, and I was talking to him for a while, trying to calm him down."

Richard's stern expression softened, his instinctive compassion for others surfacing. He leaned back in his chair, studying Luna for a moment as she stood there, her posture anxious.

"You should have informed me or one of the other staff members," Richard said, his tone now much gentler. "But I understand, Luna. Family comes first. Is your brother okay now ?"

Luna nodded quickly, her relief evident. "Yes, sir. Thank you for understanding. The insurance agent has already arrived, and everything is under control now. I'm so sorry for the trouble I caused you today."

Richard's heart went out to her, and despite the disappointment in her earlier behavior, he knew the situation was beyond her control. "It's alright, Luna. Family emergencies can happen to anyone. If there's anything we can do to assist you, don't hesitate to let us know."

"Thank you, sir," Luna replied gratefully, her voice now steadier. "I appreciate your understanding."

Richard gave her a small nod. "No need to apologize further. You can go back to your duties now."

As Luna left his office, Richard sat back in his chair, reflecting on the incident. He appreciated Luna's dedication to her work, but he also knew that sometimes, life threw curveballs, and compassion was just as important as professionalism.

Event 3

Turning Points and Reflections

The sun bathed the sprawling veranda of Richard's home in a soft, golden light as he reclined on the cushioned couch, savoring the warmth of his coffee. Steam curled lazily from the mug as the aroma of freshly brewed beans filled the air—a familiar comfort on a quiet Saturday morning. Jane, the ever-dedicated housemaid, had prepared his favorite blend, knowing he needed moments of solace these days. Richard closed his eyes briefly, feeling the crisp breeze on his face and hearing the chirping birds in the distance.

Life had not turned out the way he once imagined. Richard was a divorcee, and the bitter memories of his failed marriage resurfaced on mornings like this. His ex-wife, Olivia, was a stunning woman—vibrant, charming, and magnetic. They had started out passionately in love, but as time wore on, Richard's commitment to building Thompson & Co. Marketing Solutions consumed him. Meetings, campaigns, and late nights had slowly but surely taken precedence. Olivia, on the other hand, craved attention and emotional connection, something Richard could no longer give in the way she desired.

It all came crashing down one stormy night when Richard caught Olivia with her tennis coach. The betrayal stung deep, and heated arguments ensued. Words were thrown like daggers, and eventually, both realized there was nothing left to save. Divorce was inevitable—a final chapter to a love story that had lost its rhythm. Richard accepted his share of the blame; he had neglected their marriage, buried himself in work, and missed the signs of her growing unhappiness.

Yet, amidst the remnants of their broken union, one light continued to shine brightly—their son, Raj. At fourteen, Raj was everything Richard could hope for in a child: jovial, intelligent, and effortlessly optimistic. He approached life with a refreshing sense of humor and a knack for seeing the bright side of even the darkest clouds. Richard often marveled at how Raj managed to stay so positive, despite the turbulence in their family history.

The sound of footsteps broke Richard's reverie. Raj emerged from his room, clad in sporty attire, his energy and enthusiasm infectious. "Morning, Dad," he called, stretching his arms with a grin. "How's the day treating you?"

Richard smiled back, a warmth spreading through his chest. "Alright, son. Enjoying the peace while it lasts."

"Good to hear," Raj said, grabbing an apple from the fruit bowl on the side table. "Heading to rugby practice?"

"Yeah, but before that—" Raj paused, taking a bite of the apple. "The college crowd is planning a trip. We're thinking about something adventurous. Maybe whitewater rafting or trekking in the mountains. You know, somewhere we can go wild."

Richard chuckled, admiring the glint of excitement in Raj's eyes. He envied his son's boundless spirit and zest for life. "Sounds exhilarating. Make sure you stay safe, though. I'd hate to see you come back with battle scars."

"I'll come back stronger, Dad. Maybe even take you rafting someday," Raj joked, flashing his easy-going smile.

Just then, Jane appeared from the doorway, bustling toward them. She had practically raised Raj alongside Richard and, out of habit, still called him "baby." "Breakfast is ready, Baby," she announced, her voice laced with affection. "Please have it before you go."

Raj gave her a playful grin. "No, Jane, I'll just grab a quick snack."

Jane's face fell, her disappointment evident. "You're always skipping proper meals. How will you stay strong for rugby practice?"

Raj winked. "Don't worry, Jane. An apple a day keeps me in peak shape," he said, dramatically flexing his nonexistent muscles. The room erupted in laughter as Jane shook her head, pretending to be annoyed.

She muttered something about "boys these days," but the corners of her mouth twitched in amusement. Raj gave her a quick hug before dashing out the door, leaving behind a trail of infectious laughter.

As the sound of Raj's footsteps faded, Richard leaned back in his chair, feeling the weight of both regret and gratitude.

His son was his anchor—a constant reminder of life's simple joys and the gift of second chances. Richard had no objections to Raj visiting and staying with his mother, Olivia, from time to time; after all, Raj was the son of both of them, tied by a bond beyond their past differences. Occasionally, Olivia would call Richard to discuss their son's needs. For years, business had dominated Richard's focus, but watching Raj's zest for life made him reconsider. Perhaps it was time to follow his son's lead and embrace the adventures and possibilities that life still held.

Chapter 4

Fresh Paths and Expectations

The Monday morning sun filtered through the tall windows of Richard's office, casting a soft glow over the modern, minimalist decor. It was a fresh start to another busy week, but Richard felt invigorated. As he sipped his coffee, there was a light knock on the door, and in walked Sam Harrison, the company's Marketing Manager. Dressed sharply in a navy blue suit, Sam's demeanor was always one of quiet confidence and respect. He offered a polite smile and greeted Richard.

"Good morning, Mr. Thompson."

"Good morning, Sam," Richard replied, gesturing to the chair opposite him. "Take a seat. How's business? Any exciting news to kick off the week?"

"Not at the moment, sir," Sam began, settling into the chair. "But I did come to share some updates about our recent recruitment. I have decided to move forward with Anna Wells."

A glimmer of interest sparked in Richard's eyes. He leaned back in his chair, nodding slowly. "Interesting choice. So you interviewed all three candidates thoroughly after my initial assessment. Who were the others again?"

"Michael Harris and Olivia Brooks," Sam reminded him.

Richard's brows rose in recognition. Both were strong candidates, each with unique qualities. "And yet, you chose Anna?"

"Yes, sir. I took time to weigh all aspects. While Michael displayed strong technical acumen and Olivia showed impressive creativity, Anna had something neither of them did—a genuine blend of strategic thinking and empathy. Her responses were consistently rooted in practicality and a deeper understanding of customer psychology. She also has a humility that will work well with our team dynamics."

Richard nodded, satisfied with the explanation. "That's great, Sam. So, when does she start?"

"Tomorrow, sir. I've already arranged her onboarding."

"Excellent," Richard said. "I trust you'll provide her with a comprehensive briefing on what we expect."

"Absolutely, sir. Here's a quick overview of what I've prepared. Anna will be briefed on our core company values and her primary responsibilities as a Marketing Executive. We expect her to develop, execute, and analyze campaigns, handle client accounts with utmost professionalism, and bring fresh, innovative ideas to the table. Moreover, collaboration is crucial—she will work closely with the design, sales, and product development teams to ensure cohesive strategies. I've emphasized that she must maintain transparency in all dealings."

Richard leaned forward, intrigued. "Good. And what about her benefits? I want to make sure she understands that we value and invest in our people."

Sam nodded, enthusiasm lighting his eyes. "I've covered that, too. We offer competitive salaries and a robust incentives program for those who drive tangible results. Anna will be eligible for monthly bonuses based on key performance indicators. There's also the company's health and wellness initiative, offering free gym memberships and wellness workshops. And I mentioned our annual get-together—a perfect opportunity for team bonding."

Richard smiled, impressed with Sam's thoroughness. "Very well done, Sam. I believe she'll be a great fit here. Anything else pressing we need to address?"

Sam leaned back slightly, tapping his pen thoughtfully. "Just a few pending matters. There's the upcoming product launch campaign for **Zenovia Tablets** that needs final approval on the visuals, and the quarterly marketing strategy review is scheduled for next week."

"Ah, yes. Zenovia. I'll review the visuals by this afternoon. Have the design team prepare the drafts for a quick walk-through later."

"Understood, sir," Sam replied, making a note in his pad.

"Anything else?" Richard asked, glancing at the clock.

"One more thing," Sam said. "The partnership proposal from **EdgeTech Solutions**. They're looking to collaborate on a cross-promotional campaign. I've drafted a preliminary assessment, but I'd appreciate your input."

Richard nodded. "Leave it with me. I'll give it a close look. For now, focus on getting Anna settled in and comfortable. I want her to hit the ground running."

"Of course, sir. I'll make sure she has all the support she needs."

With that, the conversation wrapped up, and Sam rose to leave. Richard watched him go, feeling a renewed sense of purpose and anticipation. The company was evolving, and with new talent like Anna coming on board, the possibilities felt limitless.

Event 5

Turning the Page

Anna woke up early, the crisp morning air filling her lungs as she prepared for her first day at **Thompson Marketing Solutions**, a company she had admired for years. She stood before her small mirror, carefully adjusting her hair and slipping into her best attire—a simple but elegant blouse and skirt that she had purchased months ago. The outfit, though modest, fit her well, and she knew she had to make the best impression. After all, this opportunity was a chance to build a future she could be proud of.

Her thoughts were far from fashion, though. Anna knew she couldn't afford extravagant outfits or unnecessary expenditures. She had a house lease to pay and, most importantly, her brother's education to support. Their family income, though sufficient for their basic needs, left little room for luxuries. Despite this, Anna had never felt deprived. They lived a simple life, but it was filled with love and contentment—a foundation of happiness that kept her grounded.

As she arrived at Thompson Marketing Solutions, she was filled with a mixture of excitement and nervousness. The company was known for its outstanding reputation in the marketing world, and today, she would be part of it. She thought about Mr. Sam, her immediate boss, the Marketing Manager, who had seemed kind yet quick to judge. Then, there was Mr. Richard Thompson, the Chairman and Managing Director—a man with a fatherly presence who had impressed her during the interview process. His warm demeanor and thoughtful words had left an indelible impression on her, and she found herself looking forward to meeting him in person.

Once inside the sleek, modern office, Anna was guided by Sam, she was soon brought to Richard's office, where the chairman awaited her.

Richard stood up as they entered, offering a friendly smile. "Welcome, Anna. It's great to have you on board," he said, extending a hand. "I hope leaving your previous position on short notice didn't cause too much trouble."

Anna shook his hand firmly and replied with poise, "Thank you, Mr. Thompson. It was a challenge, but I believe every step toward growth requires a leap of faith. I made sure to leave things in good order, so the transition was as smooth as possible."

Richard nodded, his gaze thoughtful. "We're all here to support each other. If you ever have any questions or face any difficulties, don't hesitate to reach out. This company feels like a family to me, and you are now part of it. We take care of each other, Anna."

His words resonated deeply with her. It felt as though Richard wasn't just speaking as a boss, but as a mentor—someone who genuinely cared about her success. Anna felt a surge of gratitude and respect for the man. "I will, Mr. Thompson. I really appreciate it."

"Good," Richard said, giving her a reassuring smile. "Now, why don't you get settled in? Sam will show you to your desk and introduce you to the rest of the team."

After their brief exchange, Sam escorted Anna to her workspace and introduced her to the rest of the team. As she made her way to her desk, a mix of responsibility and anticipation settled over her. She felt the weight of the challenges ahead but also the thrill of embarking on this new chapter in her life.

Just as Anna was settling in, a young woman, Emma with short brown hair and a bright smile approached her desk. "

"Hi Anna, since I'm right next to you, feel free to reach out anytime. It can be a bit overwhelming at first, but don't worry—you'll get the hang of it quickly."

Anna smiled, appreciating the warm welcome. "Thanks, Emma. I'm eager to dive in, though there's definitely a lot to take in."

Emma chuckled. "I totally get that. When I first started, I was overwhelmed too. But trust me, the company is full of supportive people. Mr. Sam, our Manager, is great—he's tough, but he's fair. And the Chairman, well, he's the kind of boss you'll want to impress. He's got this calm, fatherly vibe that makes you respect him instantly."

Anna nodded, acknowledging Emma's observation. "I've noticed that as well. He certainly comes across as a great leader."

"Definitely," Emma agreed. "I'm sure you'll do great here, Anna. Just make sure you ask questions when you need to. And if you ever want to grab lunch or need a little break, I'm your girl."

Anna felt a sense of ease. It was comforting to know she wasn't alone, and Emma seemed like someone she could rely on. "Thanks, Emma. I'm looking forward to working with you."

As the day unfolded, Anna spent most of her time studying the company's structure, reading through the manuals, and familiarizing herself with the tasks that lay ahead. She was diligent, meticulous in her efforts to understand every nuance of the company's inner workings. From marketing strategies to client relations, she absorbed as much information as she could, knowing that this knowledge would help her perform her duties with excellence.

Though it was only her first day, Anna felt a quiet determination settle in her chest. This was her chance to prove herself, to show Mr. Richard and the rest of the team that she was more than just a candidate—they had made the right choice in hiring her. And she would give her all to make sure they never regretted it.

As the clock ticked toward the end of the day, Richard's words echoed in her mind: "We're all in this together." For the first time in a long while, Anna felt like she had found a place where she truly belonged.

Event 6

Mastering the Game

A few weeks had passed since Anna joined the company, and already, she was beginning to feel right at home. Her keen sense of observation had helped her adapt to the company's culture and work pattern with surprising ease. She quickly grasped the nuances of the office environment, and it didn't take long for her to realize the significance of staying organized.

Every morning, as soon as Anna stepped into the office, she wasted no time diving straight into her work. She meticulously sifted through the files on her desk, her keen eye quickly spotting the outdated, chaotic filing system that had been in place for years. It was a mess—cluttered, disorganized, and an absolute time-sink for anyone trying to find what they needed.

By the end of the first week, Anna had revamped the entire system, creating a more intuitive and accessible index that made finding information a breeze. She felt a small sense of pride as she stood back, looking at the neatly categorized files.

"Impressive," Sam remarked, walking into her office one afternoon. "I've been here for years, and I've never seen such a transformation. You've saved me so much time, Anna. It's a relief to have someone who can get things in order."

Anna smiled modestly, her work ethic speaking for itself. "Thank you, Mr. Sam. I like to keep things simple and efficient. It makes it easier for everyone in the long run."

She continued to work diligently, noting down her tasks each morning in her notepad. With each new task she took on, she found herself thinking one step ahead—always anticipating the next move. She started discussing the day's priorities with Mr. Sam, ensuring that both of them were on the same page. "I'll handle the client follow-ups, and I've set reminders for the meetings. You'll be ready to go right after lunch, Mr. Sam."

Sam, always a bit distracted by the daily rush, looked at her with newfound respect. "I can't keep up with your pace sometimes. You're on top of everything."

Anna was already ahead of him. She had set up pop-up reminders on their systems, making sure the important client meetings were never missed. Each reminder was accompanied by a personal note, just in case they needed to tweak the approach or bring up a new point during the meeting. Her attention to detail was flawless.

She moved like clockwork—timely, precise, and incredibly efficient.

As the weeks went by, Anna grew more confident in her abilities. She could anticipate problems before they arose and find solutions quickly. Sam had even started to rely on her for small, but crucial, decisions. She had seamlessly integrated herself into the team, becoming an indispensable part of their workflow.

On Friday morning, Anna arrived at work with her usual enthusiasm, kicking off the day with lighthearted banter among the marketing team. Everyone was friendly, but she had formed a particularly strong bond with Emma and Earl, who were close in age and shared her upbeat energy. After the brief exchange, Anna grabbed her notepad and headed toward Mr. Sam's cubicle. As she approached, she noticed Mr. Sam on the phone, his expression unusually tense and his voice low. Sensing that something serious was unfolding, she waited quietly, observing the way his fingers tapped nervously against the desk.

When Sam finally ended the call, he turned to Anna, his face marked with concern. "Anna," he began, "Mr. Richard Thompson has been admitted to St. James Medical Center. He experienced chest pain this morning, but they assure me it's under control. I need to get to the hospital immediately."

Anna's heart sank, but she quickly pulled herself together. "Can I come with you?" she asked, her voice steady but filled with worry.

Sam shook his head, urgency in his tone. "No, Anna. I need you here. You'll have to handle our meeting with Westford Industries—they'll be arriving shortly. It's crucial. They're evaluating a long-term contract."

Anna nodded, determination flashing in her eyes. "Understood. What's Mr. Thompson's ward number?"

"Ward 6," Sam replied before rushing down the stairs.

Moments later, the reception area buzzed with the arrival of the Westford Industries representatives—two sharply dressed executives radiating confidence and critical evaluation. Anna stepped forward with a warm smile, her posture exuding professionalism. "Welcome to Thompson Marketing Solutions," she greeted, extending her hand. "I'm Anna. Thank you for taking the time to meet with us today."

She guided them to a comfortable meeting room, offering refreshments and subtly steering the conversation to ease any tension. Anna's genuine interest and thoughtful remarks set a positive tone. "I've reviewed your recent initiatives," she said, referencing specific data points she had memorized the night before. "Your strategy in the renewable energy market is remarkable—exactly the kind of forward-thinking approach we admire."

The executives exchanged glances, visibly impressed by her preparation. As the discussion progressed, Anna showcased a comprehensive understanding of Westford's needs, offering tailored marketing solutions that highlighted her company's adaptability and commitment. She spoke with conviction, emphasizing case studies and success stories, weaving in examples that resonated with their goals. Her enthusiasm was infectious, and soon, the executives were nodding along, engaged and intrigued.

When they raised concerns, Anna handled each with poise, countering with data-driven insights and innovative strategies. By the end of the meeting, what had started as an evaluative session turned into a collaborative brainstorming of possibilities. The senior executive leaned back, visibly pleased. “You’ve given us a lot to think about, Anna. It’s clear your team’s approach stands out.”

As they stood to leave, one of the executives extended his hand again. “We look forward to seeing where this partnership can go.”

Once they departed, Anna allowed herself a brief moment to breathe. She had tackled the meeting head-on, transforming a challenge into an opportunity. When Sam returned later that day, the news of her handling impressed him deeply. “Anna, you’ve exceeded all expectations,” he said with genuine admiration. Chairman will be proud.

When Anna inquired about Mr. Richard, Sam responded with a calm but slightly concerned tone. "Richard will be fine. It’s just a case of gastritis, not a heart attack. He’ll probably be out by Sunday evening once they finish a few more tests."

Later, as the lunch break approached, Anna casually asked Emma, "Do you think we should visit Mr. Richard after work?"

Emma paused, looking apologetic. "I’d love to, but I have a dental appointment this evening. Sorry, I won’t be able to make it today."

Anna nodded understandingly, but a gentle pull in her heart made her decide otherwise. *I should go by myself,* she thought. She’d always had a compassionate nature, and something about the idea of Mr. Richard being alone in the hospital tugged at her.

Without a second thought, she grabbed a sealed almond drink from a popular café, hoping Richard would enjoy it, and informed her parents that she’d be staying out a little later than usual. She couldn’t shake the feeling that visiting him was the right thing to do.

Upon arriving at the hospital, Anna checked the board for Ward 6 and made her way to Richard's room. A nurse directed her, and with a soft knock, she quietly stepped inside. Richard lay motionless, eyes closed, but as she approached, he seemed to sense her presence. Slowly, he opened his eyes, and surprise flickered across his face as their gazes met.

"Anna... you came alone?" Richard's voice, though weak, carried a warm note of curiosity.

"Yes, sir," Anna replied softly. "I just thought I'd drop by to see you, even though Mr. Sam assured me you're not in danger anymore." She offered him a gentle smile, holding out the almond drink. "I brought this for you. I thought you might like it."

Richard's expression softened, a hint of relief in his eyes. "That's very thoughtful of you. I love almond drinks." He sat up slightly, adjusting himself on the bed, and Anna carefully helped him take a sip.

"Thank you, Anna. This is just what I needed." Richard relaxed, savoring the drink. "So, how's everything going at the office?"

Anna, feeling a surge of pride, smiled. "Actually, things are going really well. I took charge of the meeting today, even without Mr. Sam's presence, and it went smoothly. I reorganized the filing system, and Mr. Sam was impressed with how quickly I handled it. The clients are satisfied, and overall, everything is running much more efficiently."

Richard's eyes sparkled with approval. "That's wonderful, Anna. You definitely deserve a special incentive from the company." He gave her a kind smile, his voice full of admiration.

Anna blushed slightly at the compliment. "Thank you, sir. That means a lot to me."

She sat beside him for a moment, watching him settle back against the pillows. "Since tomorrow's Saturday, I could bring you a nice meal," she suggested, her voice full of sincerity.

Richard shook his head, gently refusing. "Oh no, don't trouble yourself, Anna. My maid and son will be bringing me food. But thank you for offering."

She smiled gently, replying, "I'll make sure to come again tomorrow, sir. It would be my pleasure."

Anna helped him make himself comfortable in bed, ensuring everything was within reach. She gave him a final, thoughtful look. "Take care, sir. Get well soon," she said, her voice soft but firm with genuine care.

With one last smile, she quietly left the room, feeling a deep sense of fulfillment. Her compassion for him had led to more than just a simple visit—it had formed a connection that, she believed, would last.

Event 7

Heartfelt Gestures

Anna decided to stop by the market on her way home and picked up some fresh fish. She had a plan: to make a comforting fish pie for Mr. Richard and surprise him with it during lunch the next day, since he was already set for breakfast at home. As she shared her idea with her mother, they both felt a deep sense of compassion for Richard's situation. Her mother immediately offered to help, and together, they crafted a delicious, flaky fish pie, infused with care and love.

The following afternoon, Anna carefully packed the pie, making sure to include utensils and napkins for a neat and thoughtful presentation. She arrived at the hospital precisely during visiting hours. Upon entering the room, she saw Richard sitting upright, watching TV. His face lit up with surprise and warmth at the sight of her.

"Anna! What a pleasant surprise," he said, a genuine smile spreading across his face.

"Hello, sir," she greeted warmly, placing the food container on the table. "I hope you haven't had lunch yet."

"Not yet," he admitted, glancing curiously at the neatly packed meal she'd brought.

She noticed the pristine plates arranged neatly on his table, likely set by the hospital staff, but she paid them no mind. "I brought you some homemade fish pie," she said with a casual smile, as she opened the container, releasing the mouthwatering aroma of their creation.

Richard's eyes lit up with genuine appreciation as Anna carefully placed a portion of the pie onto a plate. She pulled up a chair beside his bed, cutting a small piece and offering it to him with a nurturing smile. "Here you go—watch out, it's still warm," she said gently. He took a bite, savoring the flaky crust and rich flavors. "Anna, this is incredible," he said, clearly moved.

She smiled softly and continued to feed him with gentle care, pausing between bites to offer sips of water and wipe away any stray crumbs. Adjusting his pillows to make sure he was comfortable, she tidied up the area around him with the attentiveness of someone caring deeply for a loved one. Throughout it all, Richard was deeply moved by her compassion and tender manner. *What a remarkable young woman. So thoughtful and kind,* he reflected silently.

Before leaving, Anna carefully packed away the leftovers, making sure everything he might need was within reach. "Get well soon, sir," she said softly, her eyes filled with warmth and sincerity. "I hope you'll be discharged tomorrow, just as Mr. Sam mentioned."

Richard gave a positive nod, his voice steady. "I'm feeling better already, Anna. Thank you, Anna. Truly, I'm sure tomorrow will be the day."

Anna left the hospital with a quiet happiness radiating within her. There was a lightness in her step, a warmth in her heart that only came from knowing she had made someone's day a little better. For Anna, joy was found in acts of kindness, in bringing smiles to others—no matter how small the gesture.

When Anna returned home, Mr. Richard's words replayed in her mind. He had mentioned that Sam and his wife had visited the evening before and praised her performance. The compliment made her feel happy, but she decided not to mention her afternoon visit to Mr. Sam. Even with Emma, she kept it to herself for now. Anna knew from experience too much sharing could stir up unnecessary complications.

Meanwhile, back at the hospital, Richard couldn't stop thinking about Anna's visit. As he lay there, he reflected on her actions, comparing them to the dynamics of his past relationships. His ex-wife had always demanded his attention, but there had never been the warmth or genuine care that Anna had shown him today. She had cared for him with a sincere, heartfelt desire to help, expecting nothing in return. Her kindness moved him deeply, stirring something inside him that he hadn't felt in years—something he thought had long since faded.

Richard sat quietly, his gaze fixed on the hospital window as memories danced in the back of his mind. He felt an overwhelming wave of emotions rise, one that he couldn't quite define. The sunlight filtering through the glass warmed his face, but inside, it was Anna's simple acts of kindness that thawed a long-frozen corner of his heart.

He thought of his son, Raj, and a wave of sadness washed over him. From the start of their family life, Olivia had been distant—strong, commanding, and consumed by her own ambitions. She issued orders and left the nurturing to Jane, their housekeeper. Raj had grown up with a mother who cared, but never in a way that made him feel genuinely secure and loved. Richard recalled the nights he would sit by Raj's bedside, filling the emotional void with stories and comforting words—care that Olivia never provided.

And here was Anna, who with no obligation and nothing to gain, showed him a level of care and warmth that made him ache for what had been missing. She had fed him gently, every motion laced with sincerity and respect. It was such a simple act, yet it spoke of compassion deeper than he'd known in a long time—perhaps ever.

As the hours passed, Richard found himself replaying her visit over and over again. The way she had looked at him, concerned yet respectful. The way she had arranged his blanket and made sure everything he needed was within arm's reach, like a loving mother tending to her child. It was selfless, genuine, and struck a chord he didn't even realize was still capable of vibrating.

Throughout the day, the emotions swirling in his heart were difficult to express. They lingered, like the gentle weight of a blanket on a cold night—both comforting and profoundly moving. For years, he had told himself that such tenderness was a luxury he could never have, something reserved for brief moments and memories that slipped away with time.

Anna's compassion and genuine care softened him in a way he hadn't experienced in years, making him feel vulnerable yet profoundly grateful. As the day passed, Richard found himself both exposed and uplifted. In just one visit, she had shown him what it was like to be truly cared for—without expectations, without judgment, and without pretense. It was a gift he knew he would never take for granted.

Event 8

Unexpected Rewards

Monday was always a whirlwind at the office. Phones rang nonstop, keyboards clicked, and every staff member was focused intently on their tasks. Anna, like everyone else, was absorbed in her work. When the clock finally struck for a short break, Emma swiveled her chair over, curiosity glinting in her eyes.

"So, did you end up visiting Richard?" Emma asked, taking a sip of her coffee.

Anna nodded, keeping her tone light. "Yes, I did. He seemed okay. It's a gastric issue but with some complications, apparently." She paused, then added, "Oh, and he mentioned his son and maid bringing him meals, but there was no mention of a wife. Do you know what happened there?"

Emma leaned in closer, lowering her voice. "I'm surprised you haven't heard. He's divorced."

"Divorced?" Anna's eyebrows shot up. "I had no idea. What happened?"

Emma sighed, shaking her head. "His wife was having a secret affair with her tennis coach. When Mr. Richard found out, it got pretty messy. They divorced about a year ago."

Anna's face fell. "That's... really sad," she murmured, genuinely feeling for him. But before she could say more, her phone rang, pulling her back into the chaos of the workday. Emma gave her a sympathetic pat on the shoulder before returning to her own tasks.

The day passed in a blur, and after lunch, Anna returned to her desk. As she slid open her drawer to store her lunchbox, her eyes landed on a pristine white envelope, neatly placed and addressed to her. A wave of confusion mixed with anticipation washed over her. She carefully picked it up, broke the seal, and pulled out a crisp cheque for $5,000. Attached to it was a slip that read: "Incentive Bonus for the First Quarter."

Anna's breath caught as she blinked, making sure she wasn't imagining it. A wave of satisfaction and disbelief washed over her. After lunch, she waited until Mr. Sam appeared more relaxed, then made her way to his cubicle to express her gratitude.

"Mr. Sam," she began, the words tumbling out as she entered. "I just... thank you for this. I'm genuinely shocked and grateful."

Sam looked up from his screen, a warm smile spreading across his face. "You earned it, Anna. Your work has been nothing short of impressive. But I should tell you, this was expedited because of the Chairman. Mr. Richard himself asked me to make sure it happened quickly. He's very pleased with your performance."

Anna felt her cheeks flush. "That means a lot. Thank you, Mr. Sam."

"Keep up the great work," Sam said with a nod of encouragement. "This is just the beginning. But remember, keep this confidential. We provide bonuses to executive staff based on their performance, and it's different for each person. The others shouldn't be made aware of this."

Anna nodded with understanding. "Of course, I'll keep it between us. Thank you again, Mr. Sam. I really appreciate it. "With a heart swelling with pride and a newfound sense of validation, Anna walked back to her desk. This was more than just a cheque—it was a reminder that hard work, compassion, and dedication were noticed and appreciated.

Anna arrived home with her arms full of shopping bags, barely managing to balance everything as she paid the cab driver. She pushed open the door with her foot, and the moment her family saw her, their eyes widened in surprise.

“Anna, what's all this?” her mother asked, rushing forward to help her with the bags.

"Is it Christmas already?" her younger brother teased, grinning as he reached for one of the bags.

Anna laughed, her heart light. "Not quite, but I thought it was a good day to treat you all." She placed the bags on the table, her excitement palpable.

Her father, usually reserved, couldn't hide his curiosity. "Where did all this come from? Did something happen at work?"

Anna nodded, unable to suppress her smile. "Yes, something amazing. I received a bonus, a big one. It's for the hard work I've put in these past few weeks."

Her mother, eyes shining with pride, opened a bag and pulled out a neatly folded dress shirt. "Is this for your father?"

"Of course, Mom," Anna replied. "I thought he could use something new."

"You shouldn't have, Anna," her father said, his voice soft with emotion. "You've already done so much."

Anna presented a beautiful new handbag to her mother, knowing her old one was worn and faded. "Mom, this is for you," she said warmly.

Ira stepped forward, her eyes lighting up with appreciation as she accepted the gift. "Thank you, sweetheart," she said, admiring the bag. "It's perfect. You always know just what I need."

Anna gently shook her head. "You've both done more for me. This is just a small way to say thank you."

She turned to her brother, who was already eagerly exploring another bag. "For you, my one and only brother," she teased with a playful smile, "I got you new notebooks, two sets of uniforms, some stationery, and the perfect backpack."

"Wow, thanks, Anna!" he exclaimed, his eyes lighting up with excitement. "This is awesome!"

As they unpacked the bags, Anna pulled out a pair of office shoes and a few stylish outfits for herself. Her mother smiled and said, "It's good, Anna. I'm glad you bought something for yourself too."

"Well, I have to look the part at work," Anna said with a laugh. "It's all for professional purposes, of course."

Her mother's smile softened, and she gently touched Anna's hand. "I'm proud of you, Anna. But don't forget, saving is important too. This money won't last forever."

"I know, Mom," Anna said, squeezing her mother's hand reassuringly. "I'm keeping that in mind. But for now, let's enjoy this moment."

That night, as the house grew quiet and everyone drifted off to sleep, Anna lay awake. The thrill of the day was still coursing through her veins. She had never earned so much money at once, and the weight of that responsibility—and possibility—pressed on her heart. She stared at the ceiling, thinking about all she could do for her family and her company. Motivation surged within her, filling her with a fiery resolve.

"This is just the beginning," she whispered to herself, determined to give back even more. For her family. For her team. For the people who believed in her. And for herself.

Event 9

Moments of Recognition

Wednesday morning began like any other, with Peter, the peon, making his rounds and serving coffee to the staff. He approached Anna's desk with a smile. "Good morning, Miss! Did you hear? Richard Sir, is back in the office today. He looks well now."

Anna's face lit up with genuine happiness. "That's wonderful news, Peter. Thank you for telling me." She took her cup of coffee and made a mental note to drop by and thank Mr. Richard personally later that day for recommending her bonus.

The morning sped by as Anna immersed herself in answering emails and managing tasks that seemed to pile up endlessly. In the midst of her work, she caught a movement out of the corner of her eye. Glancing up, she noticed Mr. Richard stepping into Mr. Sam's cubicle. The Chairman was rarely seen on this floor, and his presence immediately piqued her curiosity.

From time to time, as she worked, Anna couldn't help but steal glances toward the cubicle. The sight of Mr. Richard deep in conversation with Mr. Sam stirred a mix of admiration and intrigue within her. He appeared more energetic, his presence commanding yet approachable.

Then, in a fleeting moment that seemed to stretch on forever, she looked up once more—and their eyes met. Mr. Richard was gazing directly at her, his expression intense yet unreadable. For a second, the world around her faded, leaving only the weight of his eyes on hers. There was something different about his gaze—captivating, magnetic, and charged with an energy she hadn't felt before. A warmth spread through her, like an electric current running beneath her skin. She forced herself to breathe, offering a polite, innocent smile before lowering her eyes and returning to her work. But her hands trembled slightly, betraying the storm of emotions within her.

Anna tried to focus on the task at hand, but her mind was a whirlwind of thoughts. What did that look mean? Why did it make her feel so... unsteady? She shook her head as if to clear it, scolding herself for overthinking. It was just a glance, she reasoned. Yet deep down, she knew there was something more to it. Something that left her both exhilarated and confused.

She continued working, but the memory of Richard's gaze lingered like a soft echo, stirring emotions she wasn't ready to name.

Shortly after Richard left the cubicle, Mr. Sam called out, "Anna, could you step in for a moment?"

She walked in, curious, and took a seat as Mr. Sam settled into his chair with a smile that suggested an important conversation. "So," he began, leaning back slightly, "the Chairman just spoke with me about the upcoming annual get-together. He wants it to be different this year and suggested we get your input."

Anna blinked in surprise. "My input? That's... an honor. I didn't expect that."

"He also wants you to collaborate with Rachel, his secretary, and Luna from the front desk. He thinks you three would make an excellent team."

Anna felt a mix of pride and nerves. "Thank you, Mr. Sam. I'm genuinely happy they have that kind of confidence in me." She paused, taking a moment to process. "Can I ask... what's been done in previous years for these events?"

"Well," Sam replied, his tone conversational, "typically, we have a bit of chitchat, some dancing, and a grand dinner. Nothing too elaborate, but it works."

Anna tapped her fingers thoughtfully on her knee, a spark of excitement in her eyes. "What if we switch things up a bit?" She leaned forward, her enthusiasm contagious. "How about a singing and dancing competition? We could throw in a round of musical chairs and some other fun games—everyone enjoys a little friendly competition. And to make it even more exciting, we could offer prizes for the winners!"

Sam's eyes lit up, a grin spreading across his face. "Now that's the kind of energy we need! I love it, Anna. This could really bring the team together." He paused for a moment before adding, "I've already spoken to Rachel and Luna..."

"Great! I'll talk to Rachel and Luna and start working out the details," she said, determination evident in her voice.

"Good. Keep me in the loop, and let me know how it's coming along. I trust you'll make it memorable."

Anna stood up, excitement bubbling within her. As she made her way to the door, she paused and turned back, a warm smile lighting up her face. "Thank you for your trust."

"Trust earned, Anna," Sam said, a note of genuine appreciation in his voice. "Go show them what you've got."

As Anna walked back to her desk, ideas for the event whirled in her mind. She couldn't wait to get started.

Anna felt that this was the perfect moment to go and thank Mr. Richard. Without giving it much thought, she buzzed the reception intercom.

"Hi Luna, is the Chairman free?" she asked.

Luna's voice came through the speaker, "Yes, dear. Why do you need to meet him?"

"Yeah.. I'll come up shortly. And also, could you let me know when you and Rachel are free to discuss the get-together planning?"

"Sure, Anna," Luna replied. "I'll let you know."

Anna tapped gently on the door, and a deep voice responded, "Come in."

She slowly entered the room, finding Richard focused on his laptop. He glanced up as she stepped inside, his eyes lighting up with an expression that was difficult for Anna to interpret—somewhere between satisfaction and a quiet appreciation.

"Ah, Anna, how are things?" Richard asked warmly, his tone both professional and inviting. "Please, have a seat."

Anna sat down, her nerves tingling with the weight of the moment. "I just wanted to thank you, Mr. Richard, for the incentive you granted me," she said, her voice sincere. "It really means a lot to me, and I'm truly grateful."

Richard leaned back in his chair, a smile playing at the corners of his lips. "You earned it, Anna. Your dedication and hard work haven't gone unnoticed. It's been a pleasure seeing your contributions to the team. This bonus is just a small token of appreciation for everything you've done." His voice was both authoritative and gentle, a balance that conveyed both his professional standing and his humanity. "And as for the organizing committee, I'm glad to see you're on board. I trust you'll bring the same energy and creativity to that project as you have to your work here. I'm confident you'll do an outstanding job."

Anna nodded, feeling touched by his words. "Thank you, Mr. Richard, for selecting me. It's truly an honor."

A brief silence lingered before she casually asked, "I hope you're fully recovered now, Mr. Richard?"

Richard let out a soft chuckle, leaning forward with a playful twinkle in his eyes. "Well, Anna, if I'm being honest," he said, his tone light and teasing, "I'm beginning to think I should head back to the hospital. One of my office staff really knows how to take care of me—I've probably gotten a bit too used to the attention!" His joke was delivered with the ease and dignity of a man who knew how to blend humor with his authority.

Anna smiled shyly, her cheeks flushing slightly at his charm. "I'm glad to hear you're doing well, Mr. Richard," she said quietly.

"Now, you better get back to work," Richard added, his tone shifting back to professional warmth. "And Anna? Keep up the great work."

As she rose from her seat, Anna gave a quick nod, her heart warmed by his kindness. "Of course, Mr. Richard. Thank you again."

She turned and left the room, her steps light, her mind buzzing with Mr. Richard's unexpected comment. His praise for her care stirred a quiet excitement and satisfaction in her. She hadn't expected such recognition, and the acknowledgment left her feeling unexpectedly proud as a smile gently spread across her face.

Later that afternoon, the three girls gathered around a meeting table in the staff lounge. The energy in the room was lively as they exchanged ideas and brainstormed how to make the annual get-together unforgettable.

Anna took the lead, jotting down notes. "So, we've got the basics—dancing, dinner, and some casual chitchat. But let's make it memorable with the competitions we talked about."

Rachel nodded enthusiastically. "I love the singing and dancing competition idea. It'll really get people engaged."

Luna leaned in, eyes sparkling with excitement. "And how about some fun games in between? We could do a few team-building activities to break the ice."

As they tossed around more ideas, Anna hesitated for a moment before speaking up. "For the singing competition... I'd like to participate too." She glanced around with a shy smile. "I mean, I did win first place in a school competition once."

Rachel's eyes widened with delight. "No way! Anna, that's amazing. You absolutely have to join."

Luna clapped her hands together. "This just keeps getting better! We'll make sure it's an impressive event."

Encouraged by the support, Anna felt her nerves turn into excitement. Word quickly spread among their colleagues, and soon, Luna, Emma, and a few others decided to join the singing contest as well. As the weeks went by, the trio met regularly, adding more details to their plans. They brainstormed everything—from the stage setup to the prize categories, crafting a list of thrilling awards for the winners. The venue and dinner menu were carefully chosen to please every taste, while a lively musical band was booked to keep the atmosphere vibrant throughout the evening. They also discussed refreshments, ensuring a variety of drinks and snacks would be available for everyone. With each meeting, the event began to take shape, and Anna's excitement grew as the vision of a fun, unforgettable evening drew nearer.

By the end of their planning, the agenda had evolved into something truly dynamic—an exciting blend of competitions, games, entertainment, and surprises, all designed to keep everyone engaged and on their toes. They went over the final draft one last time.

"Time to send this to Mr. Sam for approval," Anna said, feeling proud of their teamwork. "Let's hope he's as excited about it as we are."

"Oh, he will be," Rachel said with confidence. "This is going to be one for the books."

With one last nod of approval, Anna sent the agenda and cost sheet to Mr. Sam, confident that they had created an event that would bring the entire team closer together.

Chapter 10

The Song That Stole the Night

The night before her big moment, Anna could barely contain her excitement. Standing before the mirror, she admired her freshly cut hair, which framed her face beautifully, and her glowing complexion, a result of the salon's careful touch. The apple-green maxi dress she had chosen shimmered softly in the light, hugging her figure with an elegant grace, radiating sophistication. This was her moment—a chance to shine, not just in front of her colleagues, but also in the presence of Mr. Richard, whose admiration and respect she had come to value more than she had realized.

Anna spent the evening rehearsing *"You're My Best Friend"* by Don Williams, her voice filling the house as she dressed and brushed her hair. The song resonated deeply within her, and she was determined to convey its heartfelt emotion with every note. As the event night drew near, the air was thick with anticipation. Her neighbor, a talented makeup artist, arrived with brushes and palettes in hand, transforming Anna into someone truly breathtaking. Her mother, watching with a beaming smile, clasped her hands together and said, "Anna, you've outdone yourself. You look like a star."

"Thanks, Mom," Anna said, feeling a mix of nerves and determination. "I hope it's enough."

"It will be more than enough," her mother replied with a confident smile.

The evening at *The Grand Lakeside Hotel* was electric with anticipation. The large hall sparkled under a sea of twinkling fairy lights, and a festive buzz filled the air. Colleagues gathered around elegantly arranged tables, their chatter and laughter blending with the soft background music. At the heart of the stage, performers prepared to dazzle, each hoping to leave an indelible mark on the night's memories.

Anna's heart skipped a beat when she noticed Emma strumming a guitar. She couldn't contain her excitement and turned to her friend. "Emma, that guitar... Do you mind if I borrow it for my performance?" she asked, her voice brimming with hope.

Emma smiled warmly, the kind that could ease even the most frayed nerves. "Of course, Anna. This is about teamwork, not competition. We're all here to create a memorable experience for everyone."

Anna's gratitude showed in her eyes. "Thank you, Emma. Truly."

Anna approached the band leader, her eyes filled with determination. "I'll be singing *'You're My Best Friend'* by Don Williams in a higher pitch," she said confidently. "I need the music to rise with me."

The group leader nodded with an encouraging smile. "Understood, miss. We're ready to bring out the best in your performance. We're expecting something truly outstanding from you."

Anna was fourth in line to perform. The first two acts had already graced the stage, each receiving heartfelt applause from the crowd. Now it was Emma's turn. Earl, the master of ceremonies, took the microphone, his voice booming with a flair for theatrics. "Ladies and gentlemen, prepare yourselves for a truly special performance by none other than... Emma!"

Emma took a deep breath, her eyes sweeping over the crowd. She spotted Mr. Richard seated next to a sporty-looking teenage boy who looked remarkably like him. Richard's expression changed from surprise to admiration as he recognized Emma on stage. Nearby, Mr. Sam, sitting with his wife, leaned in with a knowing smile, whispering something that made her chuckle softly.

As Emma stepped onto the stage, guitar in hand, she radiated confidence. She strummed the first chords, and the room instantly hushed, all eyes on her. Her voice, rich and melodic, filled the air as she began to sing, "You are my sunshine, my only sunshine..." Each word dripped with emotion, and the audience swayed gently, mesmerized by her heartfelt performance. Anna watched from the sidelines, fully aware of the power in Emma's voice and the way it captivated everyone.

As the final note hung in the air and slowly faded into silence, it was Anna's moment. Earl's voice resonated through the speakers, cutting through the hum of the crowd. "And now," he announced, stretching each word with dramatic flair, "we have someone truly special. Known to surprise, to captivate, and perhaps, to leave us breathless tonight. Ladies and gentlemen, I present to you—the one and only..."

He paused, allowing the suspense to grow as the audience leaned in, their curiosity piqued. The silence deepened, everyone holding their breath. Then, with a flourish, he declared, "Anna!"

Applause erupted, a wave of excitement washing over the hall as all eyes turned to the stage. The spotlight flared, revealing a poised figure standing beneath its glow, confidence mixed with just a hint of nervous energy. She took a deep breath, her gaze sweeping across the audience, and then stepped forward, ready to transform the night with her voice.

Anna stepped onto the stage, the lights casting a warm glow that blurred the edges of the room, making it feel as though she stood in a dream. Her grip tightened around the guitar, each string vibrating with the energy pulsing through her veins. She took a steadying breath, her chest rising and falling as she gathered her courage. The crowd seemed to hold its breath along with her, the quiet anticipation thick enough to touch.

Her gaze scanned the audience, but when her eyes locked with Mr. Richard's, her heart skipped a beat. He sat upright, all attention on her, his expression a mix of admiration and curiosity. Beside him, his son mirrored his focus, their strikingly similar features making it feel as though she was looking at a reflection split by time. The connection between them was undeniable, charged with an unspoken energy that held her in place while also urging her forward.

The first chords rang out, and the music wrapped around her like a second heartbeat. "You placed gold on my finger, you brought love like I've never known..." Her voice rang clear and strong, slicing through the stillness and filling every inch of the hall.

Her gaze swept across the audience, each high-pitched note soaring, capturing the attention of every listener. With a steady breath, she continued, the words flowing effortlessly:

"You gave life to our children,

And to me, a reason to go on..."

Her voice was bold and pure, resonating through the air with a depth that seemed to touch every soul in the room. It wasn't just a song—it was a story, a raw truth, a piece of her heart laid bare. The room fell into rapt silence, each listener hanging on every word. Even the stewards froze in their tracks, enchanted by the magic that poured from the stage.

Anna's focus remained steady, yet out of the corner of her eye, she caught a glance exchanged between Richard and his son—a look filled with pride, admiration, and a glimmer of something deeper that made her pulse quicken. She could feel the connection sparking across the room, raw and electric.

As the final notes of her song faded into the hushed silence of the hall, an eruption of applause filled the room, rolling like thunder. The crowd's cheers turned into a unified chant: "Encore!" Their voices swelled with a mix of excitement and admiration. Anna, still catching her breath but feeling a surge of exhilaration, smiled and nodded. She picked up her guitar once more, this time pouring every bit of her soul into the lyrics, her voice soaring higher and richer, weaving even deeper magic. The audience, emboldened by her passion, sang along shyly at first, but soon, their voices melded with hers, creating a moment that was as electrifying as it was heartfelt.

When the song ended for a second time, the applause returned, louder and more fervent. The hall reverberated with claps and cheers. Anna stepped off the stage, her heart pounding with an indescribable mix of joy, pride, and disbelief. She glanced around, catching the smiles and nods of her colleagues.

Emma was the first to reach her, eyes bright and voice bubbling over with enthusiasm. "Anna, you were amazing! I knew you had talent, but this... this was incredible."

Other staff members surrounded her, each offering their praise. "You owned that stage!" one of her colleagues said, while another added, "We've never seen anything like that, Anna. You truly brought the house down!"

Even Mr. Sam, the Marketing Manager, stepped forward, his smile genuine and wide. "Anna, that was a performance to remember," he said, his tone warm. "You didn't just sing—you created a moment that brought us all together. Thank you for that."

Anna felt her heart swell. This wasn't just about the music or the applause; it was about the bond she had strengthened with everyone in the room. The connection she'd made, the magic she'd shared—it would linger long after the night had ended. She realized that victory wasn't merely about winning a contest; it was about touching lives and leaving a mark that mattered. And tonight, she had done exactly that.

As Anna leaned back in her chair, the cool tang of orange juice refreshing her throat, she let herself take in the lively hum of the room. Laughter echoed as her colleagues participated in the musical chairs session, led by Rachel. Anna had politely declined—her voice needed rest.

Moments later, she noticed movement in the crowd. Richard was making his way toward her, his stride confident, his expression warm. Beside him walked a young boy, perhaps fifteen, with sharp eyes and a striking resemblance to his father. There was a natural grace in the boy's movements, and it was clear he had inherited Richard's presence.

"Anna," Richard greeted, his voice carrying over the din. He extended a hand, which she shook with a smile. "I believe you've already met my son, Raj."

Raj stepped forward, his gaze a mix of shyness and admiration. "It's a pleasure to meet you, Aunt Anna," he said, his voice steady, yet respectful.

"The pleasure is mine, Raj," Anna responded with a warm smile. "I hope you're having a good time this evening."

"Oh, I am," Raj said, a smile breaking through. "Your performance was amazing."

Richard nodded in agreement, his gaze locking with hers, filled with an intensity that was both kind and sincere. "Amazing doesn't quite capture it," he said, his voice genuine. "Anna, I've been in this business for many years, seen all kinds of talent, but what you did tonight was truly exceptional."

A warm rush swept over Anna, her cheeks coloring slightly. "Thank you, Mr. Richard. That means so much to me." She smiled, then added, "I'd also like to congratulate the other participants, as they're all incredibly talented. And thank you for making our get-together so vibrant and memorable. I'll have my secretary arrange a meeting so I can personally thank everyone for their contributions."

"Thank you, Mr. Richard. I truly appreciate your kind words, and I'm glad the evening was enjoyable for everyone."

Richard smiled warmly, resting a hand lightly on Raj's shoulder. "You've left a strong impression on both of us. I hope you keep sharing your gift, Anna—not just with us, but with everyone fortunate enough to experience it."

Anna's heart swelled with gratitude. "That's very kind of you to say, Mr. Richard. I'm truly grateful for the opportunity."

Raj, feeling more confident, chimed in, "You have a real talent Aunt. Dad's right—you're amazing.

The sincerity in their words touched Anna deeply. As Richard and Raj moved on to greet other guests, she sipped her juice, savoring not just the flavor but the moment itself—a moment she'd hold close for a long time.

The energy in the room shifted to a fever pitch after Anna's breathtaking performance. The band launched into an upbeat tune, signaling the start of the dancing session. The dance floor quickly became a vibrant blur of colors and motion, as couples swirled and stepped in perfect time with the beat. Anna, now seated, sipped a cool drink, the thrill of her first-place victory mingling with the warmth of the room's lively atmosphere. She smiled as Emma and Earl glided across the floor, Mr. Sam and his wife sharing an elegant waltz, and Luna swaying gracefully with a friend. She even spotted Raj, laughing with some company executives, enjoying the evening with his usual charm.

Then, just when she thought she'd seen it all, an outstretched hand caught her eye. Her breath caught in her throat. It was Richard, standing just a few feet away, his eyes gleaming with a challenge she couldn't resist. Time seemed to freeze for a moment. Anna's heart raced. This was the man she admired, the one whose gaze had stirred something deep within her. Without thinking, she rose and placed her hand in his, drawn to him like a magnet.

The world around them seemed to fade as they moved onto the dance floor. The music shifted into a soft, romantic ballad, the kind of melody that felt made for moments like this. Richard's hand was warm, guiding her with confidence and care. "I hope I'm not imposing," he said with a playful smile, his tone light. "But I couldn't resist."

"Not at all," Anna replied, her voice steady despite the fluttering in her stomach. "It's an honor."

Their movements were in perfect harmony, each step flowing seamlessly into the next. Richard led with a confidence that left Anna breathless, while she followed effortlessly, as if they'd been dancing together for years. The world outside the dance floor ceased to exist; it was just the two of them, moving in sync with the rhythm. They spun, earning admiring glances from the crowd, and the room gradually shifted its focus to them, captivated by the chemistry between them. A few gasps of delight escaped as Richard swept Anna into a graceful dip, their eyes locking once again. The applause that followed seemed distant, a soft echo compared to the connection they shared.

"You've captured the audience," Richard said, lifting her with ease. "Once again."

"I think it's the other way around, Chairman," Anna whispered, her cheeks flushed with warmth.

Richard smiled gently. "No, just Richard tonight."

As the music neared its end, they finished with a flourish, their steps slowing until they were inches apart. Applause erupted around them, filling the hall with cheers. For a brief moment, they shared a look, the spell of their dance momentarily broken by the adulation of their colleagues. Earl, ever the showman, took the mic once more. "Ladies and gentlemen, I think we've got a new dance-floor duo to watch! Let's hear it for Anna and Richard!"

Anna laughed, the lightness in her heart unmistakable. She turned to Richard, who gave a half-bow, a twinkle in his eyes. "Thank you for the dance," he said, his tone sincere.

"No, thank you," Anna replied, her voice soft and genuine.

Before they could say more, Sam approached, clapping them both on the back. "You two were magnificent! Honestly, you stole the show!"

Richard glanced at Anna, a deeper look in his eyes. "Seems like I had the perfect partner."

Anna's heart swelled with pride and something unspoken as they stepped off the dance floor, the evening unfolding in a blur of congratulations, smiles, and lingering glances. But one thing was certain—this was a night she would never forget.

After the exhilarating conclusion of the dancing competition and the thunderous applause that followed, the lights dimmed slightly to signal the much-anticipated dinner. A wave of inviting aromas swept through the hall, drawing guests eagerly toward the elegantly set buffet tables.

The spread was nothing short of extraordinary. Gleaming chafing dishes revealed a symphony of flavors: the richness of creamy lobster bisque, the savory perfection of herb-crusted lamb chops, and the vibrant colors of roasted vegetables seasoned to perfection. Nearby, platters of rice pilaf and garlic-buttered rolls added a comforting touch to the gourmet lineup.

At the dessert station, the offerings were equally stunning. Guests marveled at the velvety chocolate mousse served in delicate glass cups, tangy lemon tarts adorned with whipped cream, and a show-stopping centerpiece of fruit skewers. These skewers, dripping with freshly melted dark and white chocolate from cascading fountains, became a favorite among the young and young-at-heart alike.

Servers glided gracefully between tables, refilling glasses with sparkling beverages and fine wines, ensuring no detail was overlooked. The hum of lively conversation filled the room, punctuated by bursts of laughter and clinking glasses. Couples leaned closer over their plates, sharing smiles and quiet words of praise for the exquisite meal. Friends animatedly discussed the evening's highlights, their plates brimming with the delectable offerings.

Even Mr. Richard, known for his typically composed demeanor, seemed at ease, savoring a piece of succulent grilled salmon while exchanging a rare chuckle with his son. The boy, energized by the evening's events, devoured his plate of creamy pasta with enthusiasm, his eyes occasionally drifting toward Anna's table, betraying a flicker of curiosity.

The atmosphere was alive with warmth and camaraderie, each bite savored, each moment cherished. The dinner was more than just a meal—it was the perfect conclusion to an evening filled with joy, connection, and unforgettable memories.

The prize distribution ceremony reached its peak as winners were called up to claim their awards, each moment more thrilling than the last. After the fun game prizes were handed out, the air buzzed with anticipation for the next big reveal—the best singer award. This prize held extra significance, as it was determined entirely by audience SMS votes, keeping everyone on the edge of their seats.

Earl, the charismatic commentator, approached the podium with a mischievous glint in his eyes. He leaned into the microphone, drawing out the suspense with every word. "Ladies and gentlemen," he began, a smile playing on his lips, "I know you're all eager to find out who this year's best singer is. But first—can anyone guess who it might be?"

The crowd erupted into chatter, names and whispers flying across the room. Earl raised a hand, signaling for silence, though the teasing smile never left his face. "Come on, you all must have some idea! Who captured your hearts with their voice this year?"

Several people shouted names, but Earl simply shook his head, feigning disappointment. "No, no... not quite," he said, milking the moment for all it was worth. The audience laughed nervously, the tension building with every second.

Finally, Earl leaned in again, pausing for dramatic effect. "It's none other than... Anna!"

The room exploded in thunderous applause, cheers echoing from every corner. Anna, knowing what was coming but still deeply moved by the overwhelming reception, stood and accepted the applause with grace. As a member of the organizing committee, she was aware of her prize—an exquisite, expensive watch—but seeing the genuine joy from everyone made the moment even more meaningful.

When the applause subsided, the evening rolled on with the next anticipated event: the dancing competition.

Earl, ever the entertainer, took center stage again. "And now, the champions of tonight's dancing competition.

As the winners were revealed, Anna and Richard stepped up to collect their prizes. The rewards, a luxurious set of gentlemen's Aftershave for Richard and ladies' perfume for Anna, sparkled under the stage lights, a fitting gift for a spectacular night. The crowd cheered once more, the fragrances a symbol of victory and cherished memories for the winners to carry forward.

Event 11

A Heart Awakened

Richard returned home with a deep sense of satisfaction, the evening's events replaying vividly in his mind. The applause still echoed in his thoughts, and the warmth of his dance with Anna lingered, leaving a lasting impression on his heart. Just as he settled into his chair, Raj's voice broke through his thoughts. "Dad... I want to hear the song Aunt Anna sang. It was beautiful. Do you have that cassette?"

Richard smiled, feeling a flicker of warmth at his son's enthusiasm. "Yes, Raj, I think I have it. I was planning to listen to it myself. It's a really touching song."

Raj eagerly went to the music collection, quickly flipping through the tapes until his fingers landed on the one he was looking for. *Don Williams.* He inserted the cassette into the player, and the soft, familiar melody filled the room. The lyrics, soothing and heartfelt, wrapped around Richard like a comforting blanket, reminding him of things he had long buried beneath the layers of his own practicality and reason.

As the song played, Richard leaned back in his chair, closing his eyes. He let the music wash over him, letting each note sink in. It was as though Anna, unknowingly, had given him a reminder. A reminder of something he had overlooked—or perhaps even avoided—for far too long. The soft strum of the guitar seemed to nudge him forward, pushing him to recognize the truth he had been avoiding.

Richard had always been the type to make decisions quickly, sometimes too quickly, but that was simply how he operated. He didn't let obstacles or people stand in his way for long. If something needed to be done, he made it happen. But there was one person he had never been able to get around—Olivia. His decision regarding her had been difficult, maybe even rash, but he had made it out of necessity. Olivia had been part of his life, yes, but that chapter was closed. Richard had never truly allowed himself to question it until now.

But tonight, as Don Williams' soothing voice filled the room, Richard felt an undeniable shift within. Anna had given him far more than a fleeting moment on the dance floor or a casual connection. She had ignited something profound, something he could no longer dismiss. For the first time, Richard recognized that this wasn't about fleeting impulses or maintaining a safe distance. This was something entirely different. This was genuine. This was real.

The path before him was clear now, the decision no longer a matter of *if*, but *when*. He knew, without a doubt, what he had to do. He was ready to make a firm commitment—not just to the idea of Anna, but to her, fully and wholeheartedly.

"I will marry Anna," Richard said softly, as if the words themselves could solidify his resolve. It felt like the only right choice, the only choice that made sense. No more hesitation, no more distractions. This was his future, and he was determined to share it with Anna by his side.

As the song reached its end, Richard sat in the silence that followed, feeling a sense of calm wash over him. He had finally made the decision he had been avoiding, the one that would guide him down a new and inevitable path. He was ready—for whatever came next.

In the background, he heard Raj singing the song softly to himself, the words now taking on a deeper meaning for both of them.

Event 12

A Love Sealed with Words

As the Monday monthly progress meeting with the Marketing and Sales Executives, along with Sam, came to a close, Richard's voice filled the room with sincere gratitude. "A big thank you to Sam, Anna, Rachel, and Luna for their exceptional efforts in organizing the get-together, and another heartfelt thanks to everyone here. I couldn't have asked for a better outcome," he said, his eyes scanning the table. Smiles spread across the room as the team acknowledged his words, gathering their notes and preparing to leave. The day had been a resounding success, and Richard knew this was a moment to seize—an opportunity where everything felt perfectly in place.

"Anna," he called softly as she collected her things, her hands moving with practiced efficiency. She paused, looking up, a curious yet polite smile crossing her lips. "Would you mind staying back for a moment?" There was no urgency in his voice, but a gentleness that made her nod without a second thought.

As the room emptied and the sound of footsteps receded down the hallway, silence wrapped around them like a soft, protective blanket. Richard leaned back against the table, arms folded loosely, watching as Anna tucked a loose strand of hair behind her ear, her expression open but cautious.

"Anna, I wanted to speak with you," he began, his tone even but layered with something deeper. "Not as your boss... but as someone who deeply values your presence in my life."

She blinked, clearly taken aback, but she remained still, attentive. Richard took a breath, trying to find the right words—a challenge for someone who was rarely at a loss. "You've changed everything for me.

You've shown me kindness, patience, a sense of belonging." He paused, meeting her eyes. "It's more than I could have hoped for."

Anna shifted slightly, the intensity of his gaze making her heart beat faster. "I'm just... trying my best," she said softly, a hint of shyness in her voice. "You deserve it."

"No," Richard interrupted, shaking his head gently. "You do more than just 'try.' You make my life feel meaningful. You bring light into everything I do. There was a vulnerability in his voice now, the bare truth exposed. He took a step closer. "I never thought I'd ask this again. I'd nearly given up on the idea. But... would you consider making this a forever thing?" He took a deep breath, his voice steady but his eyes searching hers with an openness that he rarely let show. "Anna, would you marry me?"

Anna's eyes glistened as she met Richard's gaze, a mixture of surprise and deep emotion playing across her face. She took a moment, letting his words sink in, feeling the weight of everything they had built together—the trust, the quiet moments of understanding, the unspoken bonds that had formed. She took a steadying breath and stepped closer.

"Sir," she began softly, her voice steady but filled with feeling, "you've always been someone who sees beyond the surface. You saw me—not just for what I could do, but for who I am. I've never felt so... understood." Her lips curved into a warm smile. "With you, it's never felt forced or complicated. It's just... right."

She placed her hand over his, her eyes shining. "I can't think of a better journey to take, or a better person to take it with. So, yes—yes, I would be honored to be your wife and build this life with you. Together." Her voice softened, yet remained confident, as if sealing a promise neither of them would break.

A wave of relief and overwhelming joy swept through Richard as he clasped her hands and drew her closer. "You can't possibly know how much this means to me," he said, his voice thick with emotion. "You've brought hope back into my life. You've given me... everything."

They stood together, enveloped in their own quiet world, as if time had slowed just for them. Anna felt as though she were standing on the edge of something breathtaking. "I'm just glad you asked," she whispered, her hands gently squeezing his, her smile radiant and sincere. "You're worth every moment."

A wave of gratitude washed over Richard, and he let out a soft, almost incredulous laugh, his voice thick with emotion. "Then let's make it everything we've ever dreamed of," he said, his eyes locked with hers, unwavering and filled with promise.

In that moment, as their hearts spoke in the silence between words, everything felt right. They had found a way to intertwine their lives—a tapestry woven with trust, love, and hope. It was the beginning of something new, something beautiful, and both of them were ready to embrace it wholeheartedly.

From that point on, every decision seemed effortless. Everything naturally fell into place. They chose to keep things simple—a private ceremony with only their closest friends and family. The wedding was exactly what they wanted: no grandeur, just pure love and genuine happiness.

Even Raj, with his ever-cheerful, optimistic nature, was overjoyed at the news. Richard smiled as he recalled how Raj's eyes had lit up when he learned his dad was marrying Anna. There hadn't been a single moment of hesitation or doubt—just boundless excitement and acceptance. Raj had embraced Anna from the start, never questioning the decision, as if it were the most natural and beautiful thing in the world.

Event 13

Anchored by Love

"Raj, get up, darling. Look at the time," Anna called softly as she entered Raj's room, a gentle smile on her face. "I brought your favorite—tasty egg coffee."

Raj groaned from under the covers. "Aunt, give me a head massage first, then I'll get up," he mumbled sleepily, his voice muffled by the pillow.

Richard couldn't help but chuckle to himself as he walked toward the bathroom, a soft smile creeping across his face. He had gotten so used to Anna's morning routine by now. No matter how early it was or how tired she felt, she always made sure to bring him a hot cup of coffee and a glass of water, along with a gentle hug. She knew just how fussy he was in the mornings, just like Raj, and her tender care made all the difference. It had become their little ritual, her way of starting the day with him. As he thought about it, a wave of appreciation washed over him—she always put others first, making sure everything was taken care of, even before thinking of herself.

As Richard splashed his face with water, he couldn't help but smile, thinking of how much had changed in just six months. Anna had transformed their home in ways he never imagined.

Anna, with her natural warmth and nurturing spirit, had truly transformed Raj's world. Richard couldn't help but notice the shift in him. While Raj had always been thoughtful and full of positive energy, there was now an undeniable spark in his eyes, a happiness that seemed to glow from within. It was as though Anna's presence had unlocked something in him. Raj now sought her involvement in nearly everything—whether it was something small, like choosing his meals, or as big as getting out of bed in the morning. Richard understood exactly why. Raj, much like him, had never experienced the depth of compassionate love before—Olivia had never been able to provide that kind of tenderness. But Anna? She had filled that void effortlessly, and in doing so, she had brought a light back into Raj's life that was brighter than ever.

And it wasn't just Raj. Even their dog, Rexie, had become more energetic and playful. Richard had noticed it too—the way the dog's tail wagged with extra enthusiasm whenever Anna was near. It was as if the entire house had come alive, all because of her presence.

Then there was Jane. Richard couldn't help but smile as he thought about how thankful Jane was for Anna. She had given Jane the freedom to unwind, to breathe, and to step out of the constant work mode that had defined her life for so long. It was a gift Anna had offered without even realizing it—a gift that hadn't just benefited him, but had brought a sense of calm and joy to everyone in their home.

"**Six months**," Richard whispered to himself as he stood in front of the mirror, taking in the transformation that had taken place. How quickly time had passed, and yet how much had changed. Their lives, once scattered and uncertain, now felt more complete, more settled. Anna had been the glue that had bound it all together.

Richard couldn't deny the profound impact Anna had made. Raj relied on her now more than ever—he craved those morning head massages, her unwavering attention, and her tender care. Anna had become the anchor for both of them, filling a space they hadn't even realized was empty. And what amazed Richard the most was how content she was, how happy she felt seeing the joy she brought to everyone around her.

Richard reflected on his efforts to contribute to the happiness of their home. He had taken steps to lighten Anna's load, starting with her parents. By paying off their lease in full, he had given them a sense of relief and security. Each month, he ensured they had ample provisions and extended financial support whenever needed. He had also arranged for Anna's brother to enroll in a well-regarded school, giving him opportunities for a brighter future. These thoughtful gestures, though seemingly small, made life easier for Anna, and Richard found genuine joy in being able to support her in every way he could.

But then there was Sam. Richard let out a sigh, tinged with frustration. It was obvious Sam was struggling without Anna's steady presence. He had been trying to find someone to step into her shoes, but no one quite matched her capability. Anna had a rare knack for organizing things seamlessly, bringing a sense of order and ease that everyone noticed, including Richard. The assistant Sam hastily hired wasn't meeting expectations.

Determined to address the issue, Richard suggested placing an ad in the paper and carefully shortlisting candidates himself. He wanted to ensure they met the company's needs and upheld the high standards Anna had set. Only then would he pass them on to Sam for the final decision, hoping to restore some balance to the office.

Despite these small setbacks, Richard knew deep down that life with Anna was more than worth any challenge. Together, they had built something truly special, something he treasured deeply. He was determined to do whatever it took to keep it that way, to ensure their life together remained as beautiful and fulfilling as it had become.

As Richard stepped out of the bathroom and made his way back to the living room, the inviting aroma of breakfast greeted him before he even saw her. Anna stood in the kitchen, her sleeves rolled up, gracefully moving between the stove and the counter. She wore a warm smile that lit up the room, her presence exuding a quiet joy.

On the stove, a pan hissed softly as golden pancakes cooked to perfection, their edges turning a delicate, crispy brown. Beside it, scrambled eggs fluffed into rich, buttery mounds, their creamy texture filling the air with a warm, savory aroma. The scent of freshly brewed coffee wafted through the kitchen, mingling harmoniously with the sugary notes of maple syrup poured into a small, elegant ceramic pitcher on the counter.

Slices of toast popped out of the toaster, their golden surfaces waiting for a generous spread of butter to melt into them. On the island, a bowl of freshly cut fruit—vivid orange wedges, ruby-red strawberries, and juicy slices of mango—gleamed like a colorful mosaic, adding a vibrant touch to the morning meal.

Jane worked alongside Anna with a cheerful efficiency, her hands moving quickly yet carefully. She plated the pancakes with a light drizzle of syrup and arranged the toast neatly in a basket. “Perfect timing,” Anna said with a grateful smile, handing Jane a spatula.

“It’s a team effort,” Jane replied warmly, returning Anna's smile.

Raj sat at the dining table, his legs swinging with impatience, his face lit with excitement. "Aunt, those pancakes smell amazing!" he exclaimed, craning his neck to peek at her progress. His eyes sparkled as he watched Anna drizzle the syrup over a steaming stack before adding a dollop of whipped cream on top, just the way he loved it.

Anna chuckled as she placed the first plate in front of him. "Patience, young man," she teased gently. "There’s plenty more coming." She ruffled his hair affectionately before turning her attention back to the stove.

Richard paused in the doorway, taking it all in. The warmth of the room, the easy laughter of his family, and the simple yet heartfelt act of breakfast being prepared filled him with an overwhelming sense of gratitude. He felt his heart swell as he watched Anna carefully pour a glass of fresh orange juice for Raj, her every movement an embodiment of love and care.

Richard finally stepped into the room, his voice carrying a hint of playful admiration. "It smells like a five-star breakfast in here."

Anna glanced over her shoulder, her smile widening as she caught his eye. "Only the best for my boys," she said lightly, her tone infused with affection.

Richard turned to Raj with a playful grin. “Hey, young man, aren’t you running late for school? Or are you planning to make it a weekend in the middle of the week?”

Raj, without missing a beat, looked up from his pancakes with a mischievous glint in his eye. "Dad, school doesn't start without its star pupil. I'm just giving the teachers a little extra time to prepare for my brilliance."

Anna couldn't help but laugh as she set a glass of freshly squeezed orange juice in front of Richard. "With confidence like yours, Raj, who even needs an alarm clock?" she teased, her eyes sparkling with affection as she playfully shook her head at him.

As he sat down at the table, Richard couldn't help but marvel at the life they had built together. It wasn't the pancakes or the perfectly brewed coffee—it was the feeling of completeness, of a family bound together by love and shared moments like this.

"Thank you for everything. You've made this home so much better," Richard said softly, walking over to Anna and gently wrapping his arm around her waist.

Anna looked up at him, her eyes shining with happiness as she smiled. "It's all of us, Richard. We're a team."

Event 14

A Spark of New Beginnings

As the evening drew near, Richard felt a familiar rush—an undeniable urge to get home, to be with Anna. The day had been long, yet it seemed to pass in a blur of meetings and decisions. But in the back of his mind, his thoughts were already with her, imagining her waiting for him at home.

But there was something different about her today. Richard noticed it almost immediately. She seemed brighter, somehow. There was an extra glow in her step, a lightness in her expression that he hadn't seen before. A spark in her eyes told him something was up. Richard, ever observant, couldn't help but wonder what had caused the change.

Richard approached her with a casual air, though a hint of curiosity colored his tone. "Everything all right, Anna? You seem... happier than usual."

Anna met his gaze, her smile broadening, and there was a subtle sparkle in her eyes—a glint of something she wasn't quite ready to share. Richard felt it, the shift in the atmosphere, an unspoken change hanging in the air. But he knew Anna too well; she was never one to rush into revealing things. She measured her words, always waiting for the perfect moment.

"I like seeing you this happy," he said, his voice light with playful teasing. "Come on, what's the secret?"

Her smile deepened, her expression softening. She stepped closer to him, her voice low and deliberate, each word seemingly savored as if it were a treasure. "You know," she said, her eyes twinkling, "sometimes the best surprises are the ones we least expect."

Richard raised an eyebrow, a spark of intrigue lighting up his gaze. There was more to this, he could feel it. Anna always had a way of keeping him guessing, of keeping things exciting and unpredictable. The secret she held, whatever it was, seemed to dance just out of reach, and for a moment, he felt a thrill race through him.

The space between them hummed with a quiet anticipation, each of them caught in the unspoken promise of something beautiful yet to come. Richard realized that whatever this was, it was another precious moment in their shared story—a chapter he was eager to unfold, one step at a time.

Richard took a sip of the warm coffee Anna had made, savoring the comfort it brought. They sat on the porch, where the evening air carried a soft breeze and the distant hum of life in their neighborhood. The sky had turned a muted blend of purples and oranges, as if nature itself had chosen to paint the moment for them.

Anna's eyes sparkled as she leaned back, her hand casually resting on the small table between them. She seemed relaxed, at peace, and happier than he had seen her in days. Richard reached over, gently intertwining his fingers with hers. "You always make the best coffee," he said, his tone light but his gaze lingering on her face. "I think it has something to do with that secret ingredient of yours."

Anna laughed, the sound musical and genuine. "Is that so?" she teased, her lips curving in a way that sent his heart racing. "And here I thought it was just the beans."

"Oh, it's more than just the beans," Richard replied, leaning closer. "It's all you. Everything is better because of you."

She looked down for a moment, a hint of emotion clouding her features before her smile returned. "You know, Richard, there's something special about today," she said, her voice softening.

Richard tilted his head, a curious smile playing on his lips. "Special, huh? You've been glowing all day. I can't help but wonder what's behind it." He squeezed her hand, his thumb brushing her skin. "Is it a new recipe? A secret project? Come on, give me a hint."

Anna's eyes met his, and for a moment, she said nothing. The air between them felt thick with anticipation. She let out a breath and leaned in closer. "It's not a recipe," she whispered, her words carrying a weight she could no longer hide.

He searched her gaze, feeling the shift but still not fully understanding. "Then what is it?"

She took his other hand, her own trembling slightly as she held him. "Richard," she began slowly, her voice steady but filled with emotion, "you've always told me you dreamed of building a home with love and laughter..."

"And we have," he interrupted, a soft smile touching his lips. "This is everything I ever wanted."

Anna nodded, tears glistening in her eyes. "Yes, and it's about to grow even more." She paused, letting the words linger between them. "We're having a baby."

For a heartbeat, the world went silent. Richard's mind raced to catch up, his eyes widening as realization hit. "A baby?" he echoed, his voice breaking with wonder.

Anna nodded, tears slipping down her cheeks as she squeezed his hands tighter. "Yes. We're going to be parents."

Emotion surged through him—joy, disbelief, gratitude—all at once. He pulled her into a gentle embrace, his heart thundering in his chest. "You've just made everything brighter," he whispered into her hair. "Thank you. Thank you for this miracle."

They stayed there, holding on to each other as the sky above darkened, knowing that their love had just deepened in ways they never imagined. It was the start of a new chapter, one filled with hope, excitement, and the promise of the life they would bring into the world together.

Event 15

Echoes of the Past

Richard leaned back in his office chair, letting the calming atmosphere of the room wash over him. The morning had been a peaceful one, filled with the joy of Anna's news. He could still feel the warmth of her words lingering in his mind: *We're having a baby*. The thought filled him with both excitement and a quiet sense of gratitude for the life he had built with her. He loved his family, and the thought of expanding it brought him a sense of fulfillment he could hardly express.

As he sifted through the stack of daily emails, the soothing rhythm of the moment was interrupted by the buzz of his phone. He looked down and saw Olivia's name flashing on the screen. A feeling of unease settled in his chest. It had been a long time since they'd spoken, and the last conversation had left a bitter taste. Richard's fingers hesitated over the screen for a moment before he answered the call.

"Good morning, Richard," Olivia's voice came through, but there was an obvious hesitation that immediately raised Richard's guard.

"Good morning," Richard replied, his tone calm yet firm. He wasn't in the mood for pleasantries today, with too much on his mind. "What's this about? Why are you calling?"

A long silence stretched between them, and Richard could hear the hesitation in Olivia's breath. Finally, she spoke, her voice carrying a trace of guilt. "I... I heard you remarried. I just... I needed to talk to you about it."

Richard raised an eyebrow, unfazed. "And why would that concern you?"

She hesitated, her voice faltering before she continued, a hint of defensiveness creeping into her tone. "I'm just worried about Raj. You know... he's still so young, and I'm concerned that your new wife might treat him differently. Maybe... maybe she won't be as kind to him as she should be."

Richard's expression remained unchanged. He didn't allow his emotions to cloud his judgment; instead, his tone became firm and professional. "Olivia, let me make something very clear to you," he said, cutting through the conversation like a sharp blade. "You've had your place in my life, and you've made your choices. Now, I've moved on. And I expect you to do the same."

There was a brief silence before Olivia spoke again, her voice softer but still tinged with concern. "I just think about Raj, Richard. You know how sensitive he is. I don't want him to get hurt."

Richard took a deep breath, his tone calm but unwavering as he collected his thoughts. "Olivia, you've always had your concerns about Raj, and I understand that as a mother. But there's something you need to know. You're right, Raj is sensitive, and as his father, I take my role in protecting him very seriously. What you don't seem to grasp, though, is that I've built a family with Anna—a family that is rooted in love and trust."

He paused for a moment, ensuring his words would carry the weight of their truth. "Anna is not just 'a new wife.' She is a woman who has shown, time and again, that she loves Raj as her own. And in that love, she strengthens our family, including Raj. Our relationship has created a foundation that ensures Raj's well-being, both emotionally and physically. He's not just my son, Olivia—he's our son now, and I trust Anna completely to care for him."

There was a slight shift in the air as Olivia spoke again, her voice tinged with uncertainty. "But he hasn't reached out to me. He hasn't called, and he hasn't come to see me. That's why I'm worried."

Richard let out a soft chuckle, his smile almost imperceptible, though his eyes remained firm. "Ah, I see. Well, there's your answer. Raj now has the motherly care he deserves, and naturally, he's gravitating toward that stability. Anna has been there for him in ways that are profound. It's only natural that he feels secure in her presence."

He leaned forward slightly, his voice carrying the weight of experience and understanding. "Olivia, this isn't about you or me—it's about Raj's future. And right now, that future is with Anna. She's given him the love and guidance he needs, and it's a bond that will continue to grow stronger with time. So, I suggest you check in with Raj directly—he's the one who can tell you the truth of where his heart lies now."

Olivia's silence lingered for a moment before she finally spoke, her voice quieter now. "I understand."

Richard nodded, his expression softening slightly but never wavering in his resolve. "I know this is hard, but it's important, Olivia. For all our sakes. Raj has a place in this family, and I'm confident that with time, he'll come to see the love we have for him is unwavering."

The conversation ended with a final exchange of words, and as Richard hung up, he leaned back in his chair, his mind clear. He knew he had done the right thing. His family was his priority, and he would protect it with the same dignity and strength that had always defined him.

Event 16

Tears of Joy

The soft hum of the hospital's quiet hallways was interrupted by the gentle cooing of a baby. It was a moment that would forever be etched in their hearts—a moment of pure joy and overwhelming emotion.

Ira, Anna's mom had been steadfastly by Anna's side through every moment at the hospital. Once she noticed Anna was finally at ease, she seized the moment to have a private word with her daughter, as she and her husband Henry had planned, while Richard and Raj were out of the room.

"Anna," Ira began gently, her eyes brimming with love and concern. "I've been thinking... how about coming home with the baby for a couple of months? I could help you with everything. You're still settling into this, and it might give you a chance to rest and catch your breath."

Anna looked at her mother with a warm smile and a playful twinkle in her eyes. "Oh, Mom, thank you, really. But Richard has made sure I have everything I need. You and Dad are already so busy with the bakery, and Charles is drowning in college exams. I can't add more to your plate."

She gave her mother's hand a squeeze, her voice light but determined. "Besides, you know how I work—it's all about teamwork. No need to worry. I'll delegate tasks to Richard, Raj, and even Jane if necessary."

Ira let out a deep, warm laugh that filled the room. "I'm so proud of you, Anna. You've always had this amazing ability to make everyone around you happy. You brought so much joy to our home."

Anna tilted her head, a soft smile playing on her lips. "I had the best teacher, Mom. You showed me what it means to create a loving home."

"And look at you now," Ira continued, her voice thick with emotion. "You've kept your office running flawlessly, faced every challenge with grace, and now you're building a beautiful family of your own. There's no doubt in my mind—you can handle anything."

Anna's smile grew wider, her eyes shining with unshed tears. "Well, I learned from the best."

For a moment, they shared a quiet, profound connection, the depth of their bond transcending words. Then, true to Anna's nature, she broke the silence with a light-hearted chuckle. "But you know Richard and Raj—they're a handful. I have to be clever with them."

Ira raised an eyebrow, pretending to be skeptical. "Oh? I suppose your 'clever' methods involve even more delegating?"

"Absolutely!" Anna quipped with a mischievous glint in her eye. "Work smart, not hard."

They both burst out laughing, the warmth of the moment wrapping around them. Ira's tone softened, her pride evident. "Just remember, Anna—you're never alone. We're always here, cheering you on."

Anna nodded, her heart full. "I know, Mom. That's what gives me the strength to do it all. Because of you and Dad."

She reached for her mother's hand. "Besides, you know Richard and Raj—there's no way they'd let you whisk me and the baby away without a fight!" Anna let out a laugh, her eyes sparkling. "They'd barricade the door if they had to!"

Both women shared a knowing smile, their laughter filling the room with warmth.

Richard sat by Anna's side, his hand gently resting on hers as they looked down at the tiny bundle of joy in her arms. The soft glow of the room seemed to frame her, the warmth of the moment surrounding them like a blanket. It was a feeling of completeness, of a dream finally realized. The baby girl, healthy and beautiful, had arrived into their world at St. Margaret's Hospital, through a smooth and natural delivery that had left both Anna and Richard in awe.

But it was Raj, their ever-cheerful, loving boy, who made the moment truly unforgettable. As soon as he entered the room, his eyes widened in surprise and excitement. His gaze shifted from Anna's tear-filled face to the tiny baby wrapped in her arms. He approached slowly, as though unsure that such a perfect little girl could be real.

"Can I hold her?" Raj asked, his voice soft but filled with pure love. His eyes glistened with the innocence and devotion only a child could possess. "She's so tiny, so perfect."

Anna smiled through her tears, her heart swelling with emotion. "Of course, sweetheart. She's your sister now."

Raj's hands trembled slightly as he gently cradled his baby sister in his arms, his face alight with happiness. The moment he held her, his entire demeanor softened. He looked at Anna and Richard, his voice filled with solemn determination. "I'll protect her. I'll keep her safe. Just like my eyes."

Richard's heart swelled with pride as he watched Raj. This boy, their son, had a heart full of love and a spirit that could only be described as pure. He knew that Raj would be the best older brother, guiding his sister with the same kindness and strength he had shown since the moment they met.

Anna, her own emotions bubbling to the surface, reached out to touch Raj's shoulder. "You're going to be the best big brother, Raj. You already are."

Raj looked up at her, his smile a mixture of joy and responsibility. "I'll take care of her. I promise."

Richard, with tears brimming in his eyes, leaned in and kissed Anna's forehead. Together, they shared the overwhelming feeling of love for their children, for the family they had built, and for the future they would share. The sound of a soft melody began to play quietly in the background—a song that had always meant so much to them.

As Raj held his baby sister, cradling her with the gentle tenderness of a young heart, Anna and Richard exchanged a glance, their eyes locking in a silent understanding. In that moment, the world seemed to pause, and the soft melody of Don Williams' "You're My Best Friend" filled the room, its lyrics echoing the depth of their connection.

"You placed gold on my finger, you brought love like I've never known," the song whispered through the air, its words resonating with the life they had built together—the love that had woven their hearts into one. As Anna gazed at Richard, the depth of the words unfolded between them, a promise unspoken but fully understood.

"You gave life to our children," the melody continued, as Raj, their son, gazed lovingly at his baby sister, his heart swelling with a new sense of responsibility. "And to me, a reason to go on." The song spoke of the very foundation of their lives—the children, the love, and the unwavering devotion that bound them all.

In that moment, as the song played on, their hearts beat in perfect harmony, perfectly encapsulating the beginning of their new life, one filled with promise, love, and unbreakable bonds.

In that hospital room, at St. Margaret's, they had everything they needed. They had each other. And with the gentle melody of Don Williams' song, they knew that no matter what life brought, they would face it together, forever.

www.ingramcontent.com/pod-product-compliance
Lightning Source LLC
LaVergne TN
LVHW010119170826
845678LV00012B/2486

* 9 7 9 8 2 2 7 7 9 7 4 6 9 *